Mudley
Explores
KUALA LUMPUR
An Amazing Adventure in Mud Town

Arp Raph Broadhead

Marshall Cavendish
Editions

Have I got everything ready?
So much to think about in this
furry head of mine.

I belong to a little girl called Sophie. She lives in a small town in Europe. She would love to travel the world but she has to attend school and do her homework. And so, each time her dad has to leave for work at faraway places, she packs me into his suitcase and tells him, "Daddy, please take Mudley along to see the world".

2

Mudley
Explores
KUALA LUMPUR
An Amazing Adventure in Mud Town

Hello friend(s)!
Welcome to the secret world of Mudley.
Sophie thinks she is sending me on her personal mission but I have far more
important things to do than be someone's messenger. I have a secret ambition to be an artist
and these world travels are perfect opportunities for me to be inspired and achieve
my lifelong dream of exhibiting in an art gallery!

Don't forget:
· Paper
· Paints
· Brushes
· Pens and pencils
· Note books
· Suitcase
· Passport.
  Passport!?

Let me show you Kuala Lumpur (or KL) which means muddy area where two rivers meet in Malay,
an inspired city that grew from 'tin'. These pages are my paw prints from a fantastic journey
seen through my eyes and that taught me so much about beautiful Kuala Lumpur.

3

In 1926, one of the worst floods hit KL. Water seeped in and drenched all the money in the vaults of the Standard Chartered Bank. The employees were asked to take all the bank notes out on to the Padang. They say that millions of dollars were spread out to dry across the whole field. Can you imagine seeing people's faces as they walked by millions of dollars on the ground? The police officers must have been very nervous that day.

It would have been funny to see them struggling with all that money. :)

Look! I went to a show and got on stage with the actors.

Run over to the textile museum on the Padang and look for the fabric made from pineapples. Fantastic!!!! Or go and see a show at the Panggung Bandaraya. They really have great shows and the actors are so much fun.

Dataran Merdeka

Let me show you the heart of Mud Town. It is also the most important part of KL's history. Merdeka means 'independence' and in 1957 this is where Malaysia became an independent country. It is a spectacular square with the most wonderful buildings of all types. And the Padang (field) used to be a cricket pitch. One building that stands out is the Bangunan Sultan Abdul Samad; this palace-like construction has a really tall clock tower, dubbed 'Big Ben'... but that is in London. I think they should have called it 'Big Basuki', meaning 'to prosper'. But hey, come on. Let us go and see what's behind those buildings.

Masjid Jamek

I have just jumped through swaying coconut trees and find myself here — the amazing and
beautiful Masjid Jamek. This is the site where the first settlers landed in Kuala Lumpur,
where the Gombak and Klang rivers come together. In 1909, a mosque was built here.
It was based on an Indian Muslim design. This brick and marble building is one of
the oldest mosques in the city. Interestingly, the mosque was designed by an English soldier,
A. B. Hubbock. So, there you go. And so are we ...

And this is where Mud Town started.
Right where the two Mud-ley rivers meet.

Just look at all the people! If you come here on a Friday the crowds are so big that they flow out on to the street and far beyond. It is crazy! There are so many people that they spread all the way to the nearby LRT train station. No wonder they now call it the Masjid Jamek Station.

HELLO!
I am the BFG (Big Furry Giant)... hehehe!

You have to see this model of the city which shows exactly how it looks. This amazing model was created using satellites from space. Not only that, they have photographed and recorded every single building so the models are perfect replicas. When building the models, they use different materials to represent them: wood for the old buildings, coloured Plexiglas for the new ones and solid white for future projects. It is art in 3D. AWESOME!

Kuala Lumpur City Gallery

Spot me, bet you can't?

I jumped over the wall from the Padang and WOW! found the Kuala Lumpur City Gallery (KLCG). You have to come here to understand the whole (hi)story of KL, from finding the tin mines to British rule and finally the Independence of Malaysia. Even though I love this building on the outside, the inside is even better. I think it has the biggest model city in the world, and includes a mural of KL's skyline. That's okay until you realise it is made out of 30 different types of wood from the region. The best thing is that you can leave, artistically, your memories of KL inside the Event Space. That alone has got to be worth the visit.

Went to get a drink and look what I found!
This is where the guys work on the models.
Anyone for a game of cricket?

The Old Train Station

That's a strange animal on this platform.

Watch out guys!!

Look! Another cake. This beautiful train station has some really weird architecture.
It is a mix of Islamic, Persian and Indian design. Amazing that it looks so nice.
It was built after the old train station, which had a grass roof, was demolished.
That must have been quite a contrast, changing from a grass roof to a funky one
like this. Do you know, an elephant once charged at an oncoming train and
derailed it because she was cross that another train had hurt her son.
Can you imagine jumping on a train with elephants walking around?

Look at that for a hat!

If you nip across the road, you will find a building called KTM Headquarters. Although it was designed by the same person who also designed the train station, there is a difference. It has Jharoka balcony windows. These are special architectural windows so, if you are allowed to go up, you can see everyone from the inside but they cannot see you. It is like being invisible, just like a magician in a castle.

MALAYSIA KL INTERNATIONAL IMMIGRATION 15 APR 2016 MASUK

Islamic Arts Museum of Malaysia

Stepping out of the forest I found the IAMM (Islamic Arts Museum of Malaysia). I know that you normally wear jewellery round your neck but the IAMM is a jewel you can stand in. I saw decorated pistols, swords and daggers. There was also a book that looked like a painting, and fabric of such beauty I wanted to wrap myself up like a present. You can stir up your imagination here. If you are like me and you love Lego, this place will blow your mind. It has the most amazing collection of model buildings I have ever seen.

All so perfect. But do not miss the children's library. They may not have plastic building blocks but they do have fun workshops and tell the most amazing stories on the weekends.

Welcome to LegoLand IAMM version.
Inside the museum they have loads of
brilliant and beautiful models of mosques
from all around the world.

Do you know what I am trying to do? I am attempting a
dual dome. A dome that goes over and under. You have
to use a mirror to do this (and it would be better if you
are made of rubber as well). But the inverted dome that
you see on the opposite page is really incredible.

MALAYSIA KL INTERNATIONAL 15 APR 2010 MASUK IMMIGRATION

So, after looking outside I ventured in and would you believe it....? A collection of butterflies from all over the world.

I found the word butterfly really interesting so I looked it up. And this is what I found. An old Dutch (Holland) word called them 'botervlieg' which means like butter. So, no mention of their beauty or colours??

Ohhh no!
I was just about to pick up that pebble. Silly botervlieg.

Butterfly Park

Just around the corner is another surprise — the Butterfly Park KL. This is a massive building that houses over 5,000 incredible butterflies. Think of a colour... it is there on its wings. Go down and sit in the gazebo and look around for an amazing experience of nature. As the Discovery Channel says, "Of all the butterfly parks in the world, none can compare with this one".

St. Mary's Church

Now, you have to admit, this is a funny building to sit in the middle of this muddle of buildings. Just off Independence Square lies this Christian church built many years ago. Its architecture makes it look like you are in England, but you are not (it is far too cold there!). The funny thing about this church is that it was funded, partly, by two important people who were not even Christians!

Now, pull on the Flute!

I'm trying, geez, I'm trying...

Church organs are so wacky. They look more like old-fashioned spaceships than musical instruments.

The amazing pipe organ inside this church was built by an Englishman called Willis in 1898. It was ruined by a flood and a man named James Riddell repaired it. Then it was ruined by another flood and Riddell repaired it again. Then it was damaged in the Second World War and Mr Riddell was called back to repair it yet again. The organ is now known to be Riddell's and not Willis' anymore. Hahaha!

*Visiting this square is so much like visiting England, but in the heat! :)

The Indians who first came here brought with them the Hindu culture and with it their wonderful temples. Hindu tradition remains strong even today in the Indian community of Malaysia. This site was home to one of the first temples in KL. It was a wooden building built in 1883. The new temple looks like a beautiful deep red stone jewel coming out from the earth.

I saw this man making flower arrangements and had to have one! He was really kind and gave me one.

Jalan Masjid INDIA

Gosh! I have just fallen into one of my paintings. It is bright and filled with every colour in the world. This area, also known as Little India, sells everything from saris to amazing flower arrangements to fantastic Indian food (hmmm yummy!) The smells and colours are great. On Saturdays, this place is bustling with people and the traders sell their goods late into the night. It's a shame I can't stay and watch but I am too young to be out. Let us go on. I am starting to get hungry...

So, tell me, how do I look?

Lebuh Ampang

The best chapati in town

Yummy yummy yummy!

So guess where I have come to?

If you are a bear like me and you need a break (or you are just hungry like me), go to Lebuh Ampang. This street has many different stalls and restaurants serving up the very best chapatis in town. Chapati is an Indian bread which is round and flattened and they will make it for you on the spot here; there are also sauces to spread on the chapati but some are really spicy hot, so be careful!. They look GREAT, though — yum, yum!!!!

OK, now I have eaten, let us get going.

I do not know what he is looking at,
but this money is mine :)

This area was made famous by the Chettiar community from South India. They started businesses lending money along this road and went on to start modern banking in Malaysia. So, you may ask, why all these restaurants in the area? Well, because you might as well eat something if you have to wait to borrow money.

MALAYSIA
KL
INTERNATIONAL
IMMIGRATION
15 APR 2016
MASUK

* I love spicy food but my tummy does not, so I just look at the bright colours.

BUS stop

What a racket!!
Although it is not a real bell,
my ears are still buzzing.

If you run across the road to Jalan Tun HS Lee, you will find a building with a roof shaped like a bell. When a bell chimes it sounds like the Chinese word for 'pawn'. A long time ago, many people could not read so they used the bell chime to tell everyone where this pawn shop was. Isn't that clever? (A pawn shop is where you can sell your stuff for money.)

CENTRAL MARKET

Look what I found. This building that looks like an ice-cream cake hides a great market in KL.
The market has a fascinating history. It was built by Yap Ah Loy — the city's Chinese
Kapitan (leader) — so the Chinese workers working the tin mines in KL could buy fresh produce.
The market was perfectly placed as it sat next to the bus stop that took the miners to the
Klang Valley Mines. So the building has always been filled with people just like it is today.
Some of the shops here have been open for over 70 years and they sell everything from meat,
vegetables, cheap clothing, pots and pans to even lost cousins of mine.

Chinatown

I am in KL's Chinatown. If you are a bear like me and you have a fur coat on, get ready to sweat. This place never sleeps, day or night, and is filled with people, stalls, restaurants and very good shopping bargains. Come with mum and dad though, this is a great place for everyone.

The tea in Chinatown is so horrible, I nearly fainted.

I saw this man trying to buy his chickens cheaper.

MALAYSIA
KL INTERNATIONAL
IMMIGRATION
15 APR 2016
MASUK

Haggling! Do you know what that means? It means you bargain the price down to what you want to pay. This is great fun. If you want a pair of trainers but you think they are too expensive this is the place to haggle. Say the shop keeper is selling them for 200 MYR. You ask; 'HOW MUCH??!!!' and he or she will get out a calculator and show you a better price, say 140 MYR. Pick up the calculator and punch in 90 MYR and show him. I bet you walk out of the shop with a great pair of trainers or a chicken :)

Wow!
They really are just like a modern sculpture.
What is that bridge for?

Look where I have arrived at?
This has got to be the focal point of KL. Or is it the highest point of KL? It is massive; these twin towers are among the tallest in the world. They are wrapped in metal so they shine like two candles on a cake (I am hungry again). These towers were built on an old horse-racing track and funnily enough, if a horse ran up one tower and down the other, he would have done a complete lap of the track. I did say they were massive! It has a very impressive philharmonic theatre underneath that is home to the MPO (Malaysian Philharmonic Orchestra). That is music to my ears when I have my birthday party here.

PeTronas Towers

What do you do if you want a massive building built quickly? You make it a race! So the owner, Petronas, asked one building contractor to build Tower 1 and another contractor to build Tower 2. Then they both raced against one another and the towers were finished in quick time as no one wants to be last in a race!

I am hiding in the back room of the MPO.
I want to hear them play. I just don't
want them to blow this trumpet.
Or they might blow my bottom off..!

Kampung Baru

What is this? There are no modern buildings, no huge shopping malls and no traffic jams. This very special part of KL was left to the people of the village (Kampung Baru). It is an agricultural settlement where the villagers still live a traditional way of life. The land is worth a lot of money but they refuse to sell it to businessmen who want to turn it into a modern city. I like that! It makes it very special.

There is a man named Dr Christopher Teh Boon Sung who is trying to keep the kampung the way it is, but with a twist. He says that it can become a green hub of urban agriculture within KL. The roofs of the houses should be used to plant food, crops and vegetables, using a system called hydroponics. What a great idea to have all your food above your head.

If my paws get wet, will this strawberry be the juiciest there is?

It is amazing that just behind Kampung Baru lies modern KL.

SEPANG

The Home of Motor Racing in Malaysia

Just look at these!
Knobs and buttons
and all things fun...
Not like mum and
dad's boring cars.

I feel a need for speed, so I have come to the Sepang International Racing Circuit. I know it is not very historical but I thought a change in pace was necessary. This Formula 1 and bike track is simply a breath of fresh air in your face. It has this amazing grandstand, the biggest there is, but what is really great is that, to keep cool, you sit under these massive umbrellas that look like they have come from the dinosaur era. A giant garden for a brontosaurus maybe?

Wow! Just imagine driving around this circuit with dinosaurs on the track?

Come on! I will race you!!

The real reason I'm here is because of the Go-karts. I love them! I can't go on one because I'm too small, but you might be able to. Just slip and slide around to show mum and dad your driving skills. If you can't go on a kart, drop by the car museum, which is filled with great old classic cars.

ROYAL SELANGOR

Can you see what I am sitting on? The giant mug is made of pewter. Pewter is made from tin. This is what put KL on the world map. Although we only think of tins as those things on the shelves of supermarkets, you will be amazed by what they make out of tin here. It is a must to come and see these beautiful pieces. The company, founded by Yong Koon, started production around 1885 and it is still run by the same family. The grand daughter is today the Boss. You can see her walking around whilst you have a guided tour.

Hey, I have climbed up here!

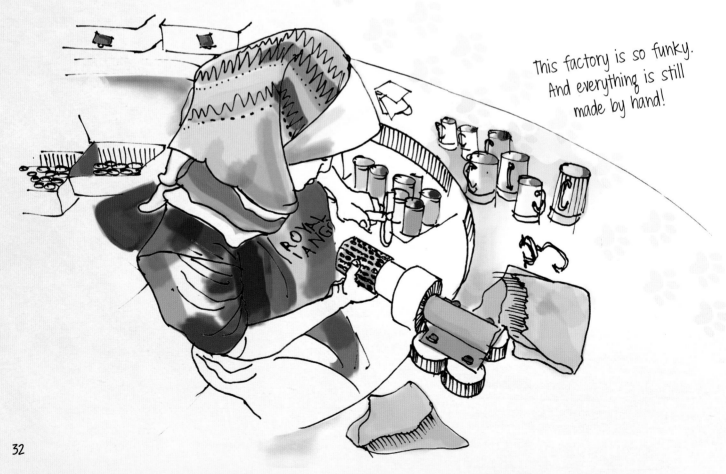

This factory is so funky. And everything is still made by hand!

I love knocking and hammering and making lots of noise but how am I supposed to lift this hammer?

MALAYSIA KL INTERNATIONAL IMMIGRATION 15 APR 2016 MASUK

school of
**hard
knocks**

And here is the best bit; at Royal Selangor they have a School of Hard Knocks. This is where you can shape your own bowl the same way they made them many years ago. For 30 minutes you can work hard to produce your own beautiful piece of KL history. Your name gets engraved on it and you get a nice box to put it in. What is more, you can even take your Royal Selangor apron home with you. Isn't that great?

15

I am a grumpy bear because I am not allowed to eat any cakes until after 2 o'clock.

I don't really know about politics so I went round the back of the hotel to the Orchard Conservatory for afternoon tea! It's not just the tea I wanted but also some of their fantastic cakes. Yummy, yummy! Sit down with a hot chocolate and look around at the incredible array of orchid flowers.

I got into trouble from running around the hotel so I decided to hide under nice Mr "Buttons" amazing hat...

16

On The Map

HOTEL MAJESTIC

With my bow tie on, no one thinks I am strange in here. :)

Ahhh, here I can sit down and rest my paws. This is truly different from any of the hotels I have been in — that's probably why it is called the Majestic, which means something is impressive in size and beautiful. This historical place is where politicians including Malays, Chinese and Indians sat down to write a resolution. The resolution finally gave the country independence from the British to form what is now Malaysia. I can easily fall asleep in such a big chair, but I can't, we have work to do :)

These houses have been made in a very special way because of Malaysia's very hot and humid climate. Unlike modern buildings, these houses are designed so you do not feel stuffy or sick with heat! They are made to let the heat and the humidity rise to the top of the building and leave through little gaps just below the roof. You do not see this idea used in newer buildings, as with air-conditioning the idea is slowly evaporating. Just like your body at the moment!

Hot air comes out from these striking roofs.

Cool air goes under the house and through the windows.

A Beautiful Malay House

This bird seemed so cross when I sat on his beak. Then I saw it was just a boat... A boat!?

I once stayed with a sculptor/artist. In his studio he had many sculptures made from wood with the most detailed designs and carvings. I was amazed by them until I came here to KL and saw a Malay house. This is like lots of beautiful sculptures all in one. Every door, window, and even the roof, is something you usually see in a museum of art. There aren't many such houses left, so you have to look hard. Get the family to go and find what KL looked like 100 years ago. Beautiful!

To be made of brick
BRICKFIELDS

If you want to explore a little more, and get more surprising insights into KL,
head down to Brickfields which has many historical landmarks. The railway line started here
and surprisingly it is still the hub for KL. A very modern and huge shopping complex called
KL Sentral sits behind me, but apart from its modern buildings, there are also many very colourful
shops, streets and temples. And there is also this funky fountain where you can get your feet wet
or pushed around like me. It is a bit like Disneyland for adults.

And here in Brickfields is where the old brick factory was located years ago.

Why is the area called Brickfields? Years ago, a huge fire in KL burnt down all the houses made of wood and grass. Shortly after, the houses were swept away by a flood. The government decided that from then on, all buildings had to be constructed of brick. The Chinese Kapitan, Yap Kwan Seng, bought a huge piece of land and fields – basically a massive clay pit (bricks are made of clay) – and started a factory to make bricks for the rebuilding of KL. And that is what you see above, the factory of Brickfields.

I came here to see the elephant fountain and was thrown around from tusk to trunk. I think the elephant thought I was a toy. Silly elephant!

TIN MINES...

I love mines. I think they are very interesting as you have to go deep into the ground to find precious metals. But what do you do with a big hole when the mines are not being used anymore? The Malaysians filled a lot of them in with water and made lakes. But for some holes, they did something very different. They made water theme parks out of them. :)

MALAYSIA IMMIGRATION
KL INTERNATIONAL
15 APR 2016
MASUK

... And what happened to them

This country was known throughout the world for its production of a very special metal ... TIN! The Chinese were the first and largest mining group in Malaya to find tin. Because of wars between the Malayan chiefs and the Chinese, the British took over the mines and brought in mechanical dredges to do the hard labour. This left many Chinese men without work. By 1883, Malaysia had become the largest tin mining producer in the world — there were 50 working mines in 1964. But today with the increase in the use of aluminium and plastic, tin has become less important.

The most famous area for mining was the Klang Valley in Selangor. But you won't see mines there anymore ... And this is why!

Can you imaging swooping down the waterways like a bucket of tin 100 years ago? :)

Hanging on for dear life here but I want to go on every ride and get my furry bum wet.

Do you see that Lego tower behind me? It is made of plastic! Or I think that's what they said...

There is something special in this building and it has to do with the light. This huge building should be fairly dark inside but it is not. The magical thing is the sunlight that comes in through the main dome of the mosque using prisms. Prisms are highly polished flat objects which reflect light in different directions. Special prisms have been placed all around the upper part of the building to refract the light from outside all the way inside the building. It is amazing to think that there are no light bulbs here. But there really aren't!

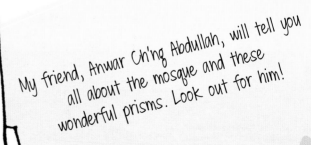

My friend, Anwar Ch'ng Abdullah, will tell you all about the mosque and these wonderful prisms. Look out for him!

20

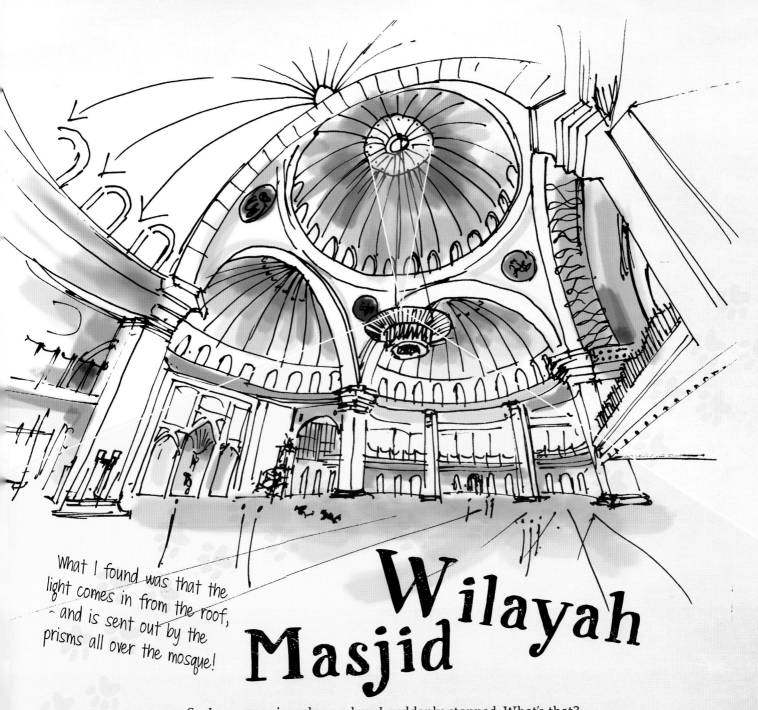

What I found was that the light comes in from the roof, and is sent out by the prisms all over the mosque!

Masjid Wilayah

So, I was running along when I suddenly stopped. What's that?

The incredible Federal Territory Mosque. It is so big I know I will get lost in it.

You can fit over 17,000 people in this mosque — that is like a football stadium!

It looks like a magical palace, with towers scratching the sky. You may think it is old but it was built in 2004 using many modern materials. If you are visiting, come around evening time when the sun goes down as that is when its magic power really starts. This is a must visit!!!

A little monkey took my peanuts and I still had 122 steps to go. This place has hundreds of macaques (monkeys to you and me) roaming around. They look nice but they bite, so be careful. A lot of people have fed them over the years so they think all the food people carry is theirs. My peanuts were definitely ... mine!

Give my peanuts back!
OK! Can I have my peanuts back, please!

So, I kept walking up, and up and up. Then I had to carry on walking up and up. And there it was...
THE GREAT BIG EYE!

Batu Caves

Breath in, breath out...

How am I going to manage all those steps???

I counted 272 steps. These caves, which are made of limestone, are so fascinating.
When you reach the top it is like you are looking out from the centre of the world. You can see the sky
from right up there through an opening and it is like a great big eye! What you see in the caves is
400 million years of hard work by nature. An Indian gentleman visited the caves and saw the shape
of an 'arrow' which he thought meant that nature was pointing to the Gods. He and other friends
built a shrine there. Look out for the statue of the Tamil God, Lord Murugan. It is one of the biggest
in the world — shining gold and towering impressively over everyone that comes.

Look everyone, it's Tarzan!

In the rainforest, most plant and animal life is not found on the forest floor, but in the leafy world known as the canopy. The canopy is made up of the overlapping branches and leaves of rainforest trees. Many well-known animals including monkeys, frogs, lizards, birds, snakes, sloths and small cats live in the canopy.

With so many branches and leaves within the canopy the animal's sight is reduced to nothing, so they have to rely on noises and songs to communicate because they can't see family or friends nearby. Any gap in the trees is like a highway to the animals that can fly, glide or jump within these natural roads. Amazing!

This is what I drew, awesome nature,
freedom and loads of fun.

FRIM
A rainforest in your back garden

Come on guys!
You are so slow...
...Come on, let's go!

"If you go down in the woods today, you're sure of a big surprise ..."
I love that song! But this is a treasure you can only find in certain places in the world.
At FRIM (Forest Research Institute Malaysia) you can find a rainforest on the outer rim of KL.
The world of a rainforest is totally different. If you visit, make sure you have a good night's sleep
and feel fit to trek 130 million years of natural history. It's slippery and hard underpaw but utterly
fantastic. The trees make up a massive vertical maze. Take the Indiana-Jones-type rope-bridge
that sways when you walk — but be careful. This is where you will understand a parallel world
to the one we live in. Awesome! That is the only word to describe it.

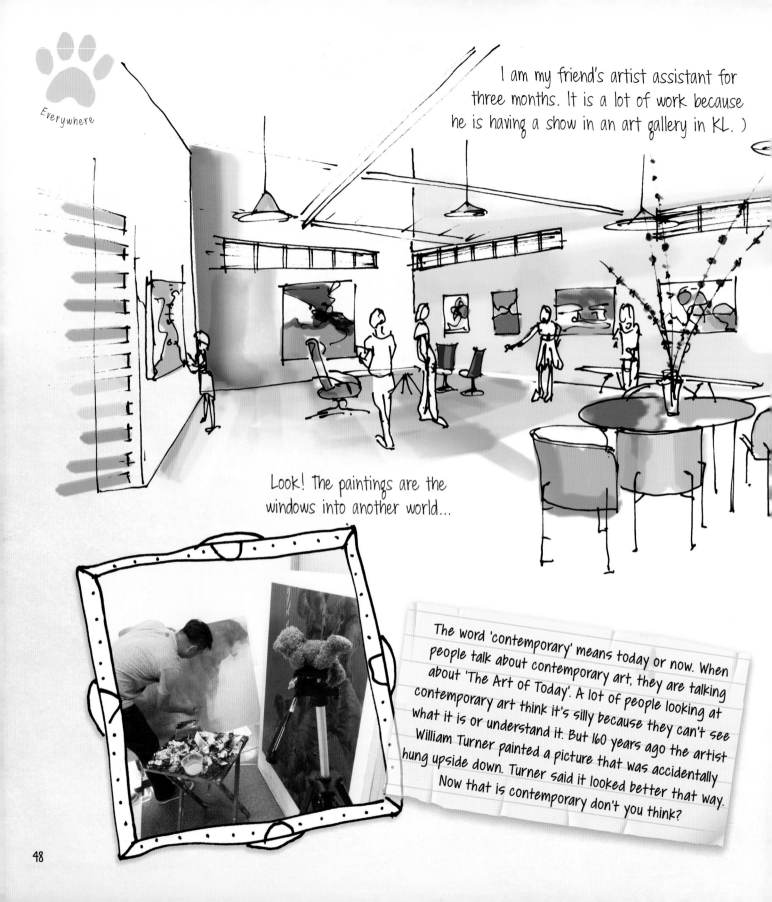

I am my friend's artist assistant for three months. It is a lot of work because he is having a show in an art gallery in KL.)

Look! The paintings are the windows into another world...

The word 'contemporary' means today or now. When people talk about contemporary art, they are talking about 'The Art of Today'. A lot of people looking at contemporary art think it's silly because they can't see what it is or understand it. But 160 years ago the artist William Turner painted a picture that was accidentally hung upside down. Turner said it looked better that way. Now that is contemporary don't you think?

Contemporary
ART

Why does my artist friend insist on putting the tops on too tight?

And finally, here I am, working for my artist friend on his show. This is my favourite job
as I get to learn all about being an artist. Getting drowned in paint and colour is fun.
I love his art gallery too, although art gallery buildings have one funny thing in common;
they hardly have any windows. This is because on the inside they hang the artwork on the walls
and have huge focal lights shining on the paintings. Next time you see a building with no windows,
remember — it is most probably an art gallery. Come in, let me show you what I am doing...

The End

Wow! What an amazing place. I have loved being here in KL but it is time for me to pack my bags
and head off to my next destination. Catching a train to my next stop. My artist friend has told me
all about the wonderful art and culture of the City of Angels. I am looking forward to that.
I hope Sophie likes what I have seen and learnt from Kuala Lumpur. I can't wait to tell her all about it.

See you soon Mud Town. Good bye!

And I hope to share the secrets of Bangkok with you.

Your friend,

Mudley

Follow the paws!
There is a beautiful and
wonderful world out there...

See you next time!

About the Author

Born to English parents, Arp Raph Broadhead lived his first 12 years in Africa and later in Papua New Guinea. He studied Art and Design at the College of Art, Manchester University, England and presently lives and works between Vigo, Spain, and New York, USA. His art and designs have been exhibited/shown in many countries around the world and he continues to search for innovative solutions whether in furniture, mobility devices or his paintings.

Published by Marshall Cavendish Editions
Marshall Cavendish Editions is an imprint of Marshall Cavendish International
1 New Industrial Road, Singapore 536196

Other Marshall Cavendish Offices:
Marshall Cavendish Corporation. 99 White Plains Road, Tarrytown NY 10591-9001, USA •
Marshall Cavendish International (Thailand) Co Ltd. 253 Asoke, 12th Flr, Sukhumvit 21 Road,
Klongtoey Nua, Wattana, Bangkok 10110, Thailand • Marshall Cavendish (Malaysia) Sdn Bhd,
Times Subang, Lot 46, Subang Hi-Tech Industrial Park, Batu Tiga, 40000 Shah Alam,
Selangor Darul Ehsan, Malaysia.

Marshall Cavendish is a trademark of Times Publishing Limited

National Library Board, Singapore Cataloguing-in-Publication Data
Name(s): Broadhead , Arp Raph.
Title: Mudley explores Kuala Lumpur : an amazing adventure in Mud Town / Arp Raph Broadhead.
Description: Singapore : Marshall Cavendish Editions, 2016.
Identifier(s): OCN 948339518 | ISBN 978-981-47-2194-3 (paperback)
Subject(s): LCSH: Kuala Lumpur (Malaysia—Description and travel—Juvenile literature. |
Kuala Lumpur (Malaysia—History—Juvenile literature.
Classification: DDC 915.95104—dc23

Printed in Singapore by Fabulous Printers Pte Ltd